The
Party

and other sensuous
distractions

Marnie

The Party

By Marnie

It was definitely a last-minute idea: something that occurred to me as I was shopping one morning. It had been awhile, I thought, since I'd invited the whole gang over.

As our lives had changed - and children began entering many of our friend's lives - we found ourselves getting together less. Gone were the all-night bull sessions that last until dawn; the bong and beer fueled parties that left us bleary-eyed and giddy for the rest of the week. I missed my good friends! Most of our exchanges these days appeared on Facebook : I would put out a statement and 19 people would click "like".

The age of social interaction was dead.

I phoned Larry. "I want to throw a party," I said.

He was used to my idiosyncracies. "When?" he said.

"Tonight. A little BBQ with just a few couples."

"A barbecue implies food," he said.

"I'm in the supermarket right now."

"Who's coming over?" he said. That's what I loved about my husband the most – he was always up for one of my crazy ideas.

"I dunno. I haven't called anyone yet."

"Better get busy," Larry dead-panned. "We're losing light."

Funny guy. I dialed Shelly first. She was my oldest and dearest. Predictably, she was up for anything. "What can I bring?" she said.

"Whatever you feel like drinking," I shrugged. "I haven't really thought it through. Just come on over."

I got a few voicemails before connecting with Nancy. She was enthused but said that she would first run it past her husband.

All told, I reached out to five couples – I thought that would be a nice round number. Then I quickly checked out and hurried home to get ready.

After all the preparation (having a party can be costly and a lot of work), we were ready. Larry popped into the shower while I slipped into a light sun dress.   My legs looked tan and shapely as I turned in the mirror. I hadn't had any children myself, and my flat tummy and rockin' ass testified that I hadn't lost too much in the years since college.

I caught a glimpse of my husband in he mirror behind me: he was soaping up his nice fat cock. Except for a slight paunch, he too had managed to maintain his old college quarterback frame. All in all, I thought, we were holding together nicely.

Larry checked on the ice situation and set up his small bar outside on the patio, while I busied myself heating the snacks which consisted of cocktail weenies and small crab cakes.

The first guests began to arrive around six-thirty. Betty and Dan, two of my oldest and dearest friends. Nancy and Paul arrived with Jules and Russ. Now it was beginning to look like a party.

There were eight of us, four couples. A nice comfortable number for an intimate dinner or an informal get-together.

I had no idea how intimate the party was about to become.

We settled around an outdoor table. Larry took the meat from the grill and began carving it while our guests nibbled on snacks and sipped beer. I slipped into the house to get a tray of rum jello shots I left cooling in the refrigerator. When I returned I was in for the shock of my life!

Larry, my husband, was seated at the edge of the pool with Nancy's voluptuous tits in his mouth. Well, the left one at least.

"She dared me," he said when he saw me standing there with my mouth open. "That's true," said Dan. 'It was a bona fide dare."

Russ – who evidentally had been drinking before he arrived – ran over to our pool's edge and stood on the edging. "Last one in is a rotten egg," he said, pulling his pants off with a deft flourish. I couldn't believe it. I was watching one of my dearest friend's husbands flash his dick!

I must have stood there, stone silent, for a long time. Paul took the jello shots out of my arms and set them on a table. "Come on," he said. "You can't be the only hold out."

Before I could react, Nancy was imploring everyone to join her in the pool.

She stood on the edge of our pool and stripped down to panty and bra, then did a perfect swan dive into the deeper end. Two others seemed to join her immediately, even Larry.

Hands reached up to carry me, I felt lifted on a cloud, I swear, as I was delivered into the drink. Paul was beside me, pressing his hungry lips to mine. I could smell the peppers and spices from some of my appetizers on his lips.

"Wait-" I gasped, craning my neck to see what the others were up to. I must say, I was a little shocked to see our friend's in various states of undress, engaged in behavior that would not have been given a G-rating!

"I'm not a great swimmer," I said nervously as Paul pawed at my wet black dress.

"I was counting on that," he said.

His strong forearm encircled my waist as he drew me down to the faux rock waterfall we'd installed last summer. From the corner of my eye, I saw that Nancy was sitting cross-legged and nude from the waist up by the pool's steps. Larry was licking her thighs and slowly working her panties off.

Paul had stripped me to the waist; my little black dress lay uselessly beside me in the water like a life saver the kids use. Deftly, he unhooked my black bra and began working his tongue over my hard pink nipples.

I couldn't even tell if I was wet or it was just pool-water as he worked his hand into my g-string and began working my sopping pussy with his thumb.

You see, I'd always had my eye on Paul. I think he felt it too. It was only a matter of time before we'd find ourselves in exactly this situation!

My arms hooked Paul's neck (I was really not a great swimmer, that was true) and our legs entangled under the churning water of the rock falls. When I brushed against him, I could feel how rock hard he had become as his cock strained against the thin material of his boxers.

I wanted Paul inside me, there was no denying it now!

Our lips clashed as we kissed. Out of the corner of my eye, I saw Betty and Russ together, on the patio. Their lips locked as his fingers moved south – across her taut belly and firm thighs, over her mons venus and slipping seductively (first one, then the other) into her juicy pussy.

Betty moaned as Russ' fingers began to move inside her vagina, instantly arousing her. I was mesmerized, I couldn't take my eyes off them – even as Paul ripped my g-string away.

Russ was fully erect now. He held Betty in a spoon fashion, his rock hard cock lay on her bare tanned buttock. His hand reached around her to cup her breast as he inhaled her faintly perfumed neck. With very little effort, Russ could have exploded his hot sticky foam across Betty's thigh. But he needed more from this opportunity: he lifted her left leg and teased her pussy lips with the crown of his dick.

She shifted her weight to allow his throbbing shaft inside and moaned as she felt his length enter her roughly from behind.

Paul held my shivering bare shoulders with his large hands. He kissed me tenderly as he slid his shaft to the hilt inside my hot vaginal barrel.

I gasped as he lifted my legs to wrap around his waist. He pinned me against the rock wall, pistoning his cock into my eager hole. "Yes, fuck me Paul," I hissed into his ear, as if we'd been lovers for decades.

His shaft seemed to swell inside my tender pink walls as he hunched his shoulders and exploded hot cum inside me. "GGGG—nnnn," he stammered. "Too soon, too soon."

But he was at the point of no return. I could feel wave after wave of hot sticky cum fill me as Paul emptied his seed inside my tight snatch.

Too soon? Perhaps.

But he had 3 more opportunities that night as I drained that man dry. From the tangle of bodies that the sunrise exposed, lying spent and weary around my backyard pool, I'm going to guess that it was one of the most fondly remembered get-togethers in our friend's history.

And as for the few others who ignored my call, or couldn't make it?

Well, they just don't know what they missed. Do they?

-30-

Marnie

The
Stockboy

erotica by Marnie

&&&

I was convinced the boy was a lunkhead. He did everything I asked of course, and he never talked back.

But when I tried to engage him in the weather, or about something in the news, he seemed clueless.

"I never got around to buying a tv," he'd say. "Don't have much use for a radio."

Clueless. A piece of work with broad shoulders and well-chisled biceps. Not that he ever gave me reason to complain about his performance.As a stockboy,he was terrific. Emptied the skews, re-stocked shelves, maintained
inventory like an overseer to the manor born. I spent many idle hours waiting on customers and watching Axl (even his name was slightly ridiculous) work.

I <u>loved</u> to watch Axl work.

He always wore a shredded gray wife beater tee-shirt: I guessed it must be his lucky shirt because he never seemed to be without it (even when he wore a nicer shirt over it, you would always see the remnant of that gray rag underneath.

Because he worked outdoors lifting heavy boxes of paint and furniture it was always a pleasure to watch Axl's musculature as he strained under each week's shipment.

Troy the driver was in the union – he'd lift the boxes slightly or tilt them in Axl's direction but he worked scrupulously to avoid heavy lifting.

Axl did most of the grunt work. Easily, handily, grunting slightly, muscles rippling. With Debbie out front watching the register, and Axl beginning to check in the skids and re-check the inventory of the backroom, Troy sat or pretended to be heavily immersed in work.

Always in the back of my mind, I was sure that Axl was aware of the effect his little performance was having on me. The full time I watched him work, I had to stop into the ladies room to finger myself. It soon became a regular practice, every Wednesday in the backroom.

I was sure that Axl knew because he'd always tug on the bathroom door to announce that Troy was backing his truck out and needed a signature.

Thursday was Debbie's 'early' night. She left the store at six: Axl and I remained until nine. I handled the customers while he continued to put away our stock.

By eight o'clock, the customer's had evaporated and it was
looking to be one long last hour.
I tried to engage Axl in small talk:
"Are you seeing anyone these days?" I asked, casually enough.
"Me? No," he said. "There was a girl but she moved to
Spokane."
"Do you miss her?"
For the first time since I'd known him, I saw emotion in Axl's
face. Just a faint glimmer, like a passing rain cloud.
"We were a good fit," he shrugged.
Even the store's garish fluorescent lighting couldn't hide a
small tear in the big lug's right eye. I wanted to hug the
boy. I don't know what came over me, some maternal urge to
wrap my arms around him and console him.
"You must have really cared for her," I said, crossing to
where he was sitting on the countertop with his legs dangling
over the side. I pressed my chest tightly against his.
"I loved her," he said with a small choke in his throat.
You know how sometimes a hug goes on uncomfortably long? Those
hugs that reach a point where someone - dear God - has to
unclench?
Well , this wasn't one of them. I felt like I could hold onto
Axl's strong shoulders until we melted together.
I could feel his heart beating strongly against my hardening
nipples. His shoulder and back were heavily muscled - it felt
like I was running my hands over a machine.
"Your hair smells nice," he said as he burrowed his face into
the side of my neck. I was getting aroused and I could tell -
from the thick rising tool in his pants - that the feeling was
mutual.
Axl slipped down from the counter and lifted me to his waist
with his hands under my buttocks. I'm sure at 115 pounds that
this was one package the lunk-head didn't mind dead-lifting!
He carried me over to the carpet and flooring section. He
yanked a section of white shag from its 12 foot roller, and
laid me down on the soft carpet. Already, I was wet with
anticipation. He left to partially turn out the lights in the
store and to lock the front door. There were always a few
brains who would park and try yanking the door anyway - that
was just the nature of the beast.
When Axl returned, he had taken off his shirt. His broad
shoulders and massive corded arms and back almost took my
breath away. From here on, I resolved, we would have to have a
no shirt policy!
He lay down beside me on the soft carpet and took me in those
giant arms. His kisses were surprisingly gentle.
My fingers wound through his thick tangle of curly hair as I
drew his face to mine. I don't think I've ever wanted a man as
much as I wanted Axl tonight.
I could feel him pressing his manhood against me. My fingers
tightened against his buttocks, kneading the hard flesh like

bakery dough. He pinned me against the soft carpet with his aching loins while he struggled to remove my blouse. My breasts spilled over the tops of my bra and Axl's hot breath hovered over them like they were warm loaves of bread from the oven.

His tongue worked my nipples as he stripped me completely of my clothes, yanking at my dress like an obstacle he had no intention of being stopped by.

He squirmed from his jeans and lay across me, the two of us completely and unashamedly naked now. I could feel his cock strengthen and harden against my right leg.

He held my arms above my head with one strong hand, while his other cupped my chin and brought my kisses closer to his waiting lips. For a man as hard and well-muscled as Axl was, his lips were surprisingly soft.

The hand on my chin dropped to my left breast. He kneaded my soft full tit like a bread loaf, flicking his thumb and forefinger over my nipple until it began to harden.

His rough hands ran over my sides and belly, until he found my sopping panties. Axl's fingers dug into my soft aching pussy, first over the cotton undies and then peeling those aside as they teased my waiting lips open.

I gasped suddenly as he dug his index finger into my gash. He rubbed my clit with his thumb as he drove his index and ring finger deeper into my vaginal barrel.

My head was swimming as he showered me with deep soulful kisses while his hands played over my squirming body.

Axl worked his mouth down my stomach to the insides of my thighs. I squirmed under his soulful touch as the tip of his tongue flicked my eager clit. He put his mouth fully against my private area, covering me with his hot breath and warm, searching tongue. He inched his squirming thick tongue into my hot waiting gash.

He lifted my buttocks with both hands, drawing me closer to his devouring mouth.

Waves of sensation swept over me as I fell back gasping. Axl made me cum easily with his mouth. My hair swept back against the carpet as my head swooned and I lowered myself from my elbows (where I was watching the stock boy eating me) to lie flat on my back - staring up at the reserve lights that left a soft grey glow on the scene below. He entered me without prelude, hammering his thick hard penis against the walls of my pink vaginal love tube with reckless abandon. He grunted as his hands gripped my bare ticklish hips, pounding against me like a piston. My vision swam like I was underwater as Axl drove his shaft into my throbbing hole. His balls slapped against me noisily as I moaned under his confident pummelling. "Grr-nnn," he groaned suddenly. I could feel his cock throb as he came inside me, gallons of thick sticky cum painting my vaginal walls.

Axl collapsed against me, his thick arms limp as I ran my red
polished fingers against them. "That was too good," he said as
he summoned the strength to take me again.

-30-

Bone-us Story…

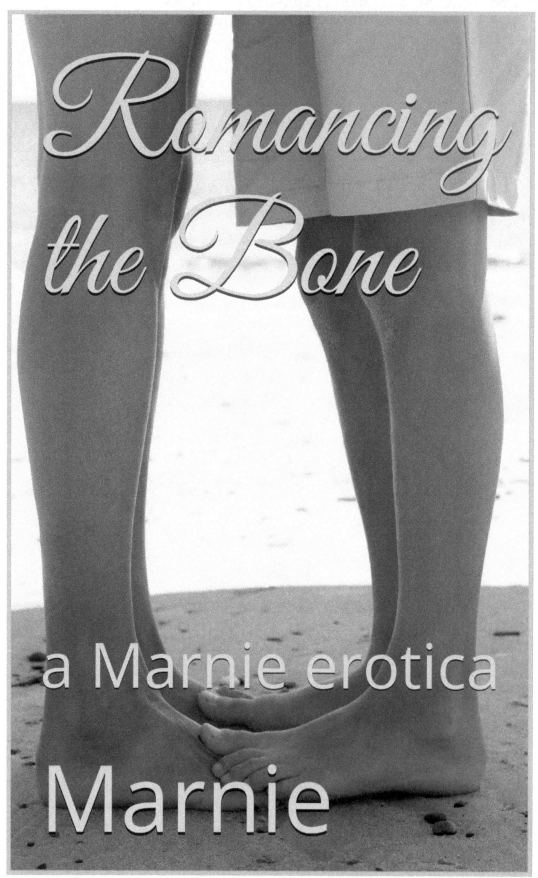

Romancing the Bone

a Marnie erotica

Marnie

I don't even know why I said yes. It was the oddest invitation
I'd ever received and I think it caught me so far off-guard
that my only reaction was to accede to a request that made me
uncomfortable the moment it left my lips.

We were talking about the beach. Our strangest beach stories
revealed. There were 4 of us altogether, a strange last-minute
invitation to Saturday brunch. None of us really knew each
other all that well. Someone suggested a skinny dip and it
reminded me of my college years. I think we were all feeling a
little light-headed as we piled into one car and drove off to
the nearest lake.

There was my girl-friend from work, Nancy, to my left. She was
cute as hell, not that I'd ever entertained any notion of
seeing her in any but the most professional light. Brad was
driving: I have to tell you, I've never met anyone named Brad
that I had the slightest desire to tangle in bed with but this
one was different. He had dark curly hair and a sensuous twist
to his upper lip that reminded me of Paul Newman or Marlon
Brando in their youth.

I had asked Benny, the kid from accounting. There was
something about Benny: when he moved, he was lithe like a
cougar. Otherwise he was your typical nerd: glasses, pencil
protector, slightly sibilant "S" when he spoke. I was dying to
see him naked.

We got to the beach around 1. The highest point of the
afternoon, we were all sure to get a sun-burn. I even thought
of mentioning it but I thought the others would laugh.

Nancy spread a blanket on a section of sand fairly removed
from the populace. "I have to laugh," said Brad. "Where do all
of these people come from? Doesn't anyone work anymore?"

It was true. Though we'd picked a section away from the rest
of the beach – almost but not nearly quite deserted – I could
see there were dozens of nude people frolicking in the not too
distant distance.

Benny, the kid from accounting, was the first to pull off his
pants. I have to say we were ALL quite impressed! The kid was
packing some heat after all.

Nancy's tits bounced into view as I tried to recover from
Benny's giant cock. She folded her blouse demurely on the
blanket as Brad pulled off his shirt.

For a guy who hardly hit the gym, Brad had a firm athletic
upper torso. His arms were more defined than I expected, his
stomach taut and covered with the same curly hair we could see
in plain evidence on his head.

I was wearing a light brown dress, and I pulled it over my
head. I could hear Benny say 'whoa' lightly as I slipped off

my bra. I was glad that I'd shaved recently so my slit shone perfectly in the bright sunlight like a small clam.

The four of us linked arms and hiked to the water. The chill of the ocean took me a little off-guard and I gasped as it ran through my legs and splashed my flat stomach.

Benny must have thought I was slipping because he took the opportunity to slip his hand behind me, propping up the small of my back with his firm strong hand.

I couldn't stop looking at the chunk of meat hanging between his legs like a salami in a deli window.

"It's colder than I thought," I said, shivering slightly.

"Hold me close," said Benny. "We can trade each other's body temperature."

Well, that was a new one. I was beginning to re-assess this accountant nerd. The kid had some moxie. He pulled me closer to him as a wave crashed against our sides. I could feel the head of his throbbing cock playing at my golden portal.

Did he not know that I could feel him in all of his goofy glory dangling that magnificent meat pole against my pink love gash? Did he think that I would be so terrified of the waves that I would ignore his cock resting comfortably between my thighs?

I rubbed my pussy lips against the top of his shaft. Pretending that it was the ebb and flow of the water that moved my body in a sort of slow sensuous rhythm.

From the corner of my eye, I saw Brad suckling Nancy's meat wagons. I let my head drop back and felt Benny lightly kissing my neck.

I have to admit I was getting turned on. Not that he was my type at all (at all) but there was something innocent and yet not so innocent about our slow grind under the curtain of waves in a giant ocean. I felt him lift my right leg up over his haunch, and gasped as he drove his cock deep inside me, in full view of anyone perceptive enough to be watching.

Over and over Benny pounded my tight pussy lips like the tide pounding the sandy shore. His breathing came closer and heavier as I felt his cock brush my vaginal walls and contract with the pent-up juice he must have saved up as he fantasized about a moment just like this.

I held onto his pale shoulders as he pumped inside my throbbing pussy. My tits slapped his hard chest as he grunted heavily and erupted inside me. He held me for a long time after that, just breathing heavily and holding on, the two of us -a man and a woman - alone in the ocean, spent.

 Nancy was bent over, her chin in the surf, as Brad plowed into her doggy-style. I could see her eyes roll back in her head as she climaxed, and Brad too treated her to a creampie in the rollicking surf.

We drove back in silence. This was one ocean brunch that we all intended to repeat again before summer was through.

Marnie M

Forced!

She was stunning. He loved to watch her dance. Every afternoon
at 4:30 he made a special trip from his office to the little
coffee shop on the corner. Armed with a cruller and a
steaming cup of coffee, he'd stake out a little table in the
window and direct his gaze to the second floor of the studio
across Madison.
The concentration as she lifted her delicate ankle to the
barre was intense. Her right arm swung gracefully over her
head, hand turned gracefully as she lowered her leg and
executed a beautiful tendu.
Then she swung her leg back into an arabesque.
At nights, he had learned the terms so that he could watch his
graceful swan as she practiced every afternoon at half past 4.
As she pranced and galloped and leapt across the spare studio
of wood and glass in a nameless rehearsal studio, across
Madison and this dull little coffee spot, he had fallen in
love.
 Of course it was unrequited.
He began following her, Not only for his afternoon coffee
break but on weekends and after work. She was a creature of
habits: shopping the same vegan stores for produce, coffee at
the same little groceria. She didn't seem to have a steady
job, so he guessed that she was married or a student living
with her parents or kept.
She had incredible style sense, preferring large elegant
scarves over almost most of her blouse tops.

*I began staying a bit longer. Shrinking back a little into the
lengthening shadows of the buildings as she left the building
at 4 pm and headed south . I followed at a safe distance,
watching her leggings under her long skirt as she moved
rapidly through pedestrian traffic.
Gradually he learned where she lived, spoke with a few
neighbors and found she lived alone.*

She had her hair done once a week, nails every two. A creature
of habit. He followed her to each appointment, pretending to
rummage through his in box even as he snapped her picture.
He would arrange the gallery of photographs in his apartment.
Gradually he created a respectable peaen to his beloved in the
corner of his kitchenette.
He couldn't be sure when he decided that following her wasn't
enough. He had to possess her. She would, he was certain,
learn to love him.
He decided to kidnap her.
She was on her way to her rehearsal hall when he saw his
opportunity. "Are you a dancer?" he said, standing behind her
in the coffee line.

"I am," she smiled. She turned back to the menu.
"I could tell," he said. "You have fine bone structure. I used
to be a choreographer."
"Really?" she said, turning to look at him now. A little more
interested.

*I dropped a few names - Fosse, Balanchine. In short order, we
were sitting at a small table in the back of the room. I plied
her with compliments. Eventually she felt comfortable enough
with me to let me walk her to her rehearsal.*
*I watched from the street below as she moved from a demi plie
to a grand jete. She was like a magnificent racehorse, moving
through her paces with grace and inner strength.*
*When she came down to street level, towel over her neck,
leggings against the cold, I followed. In the lobby of her
building, she fumbled in her pocketbook for her pass card.*
*I slipped in behind her as the door buzzed. "What th-" she
whirled toward me, and almost smiled in a blink of recognition
before recovering and flashing those beautiful grey eyes.*
*"You can't be here," she said uselessly as I gripped her arm
and advised her to keep walking.*
*I'd been here earlier, concluded there were no working
cameras or security of any kind. We marched to the elevator. I
pressed her floor.*
"What are you doing here?" she said coldly.
*I reached for her pocketbook and fiddled for her apartment
key. She was surprisingly tidy, and I was able to fish out the
keys almost at once.*
"I'll scream," she threatened.
"No, you won't," I said coldly.
*She didn't scream. Just the same, I tied her mouth with a robe
sash and lashed her arms to the headboard of her bed.*
*She watched me curiously, half-expecting me to ransack her
cabinets, to steal the little costume jewelry she managed to
accrue.*
*I tied her legs to the footboards, spread eagle-style, but it
wasn't until I began to slice her clothes away with a small
switchblade I'd purchased on Canal Street that she began to
squirm uncomfortably. Her eyes began to register real fear as
I caressed her soft skin.*
*She was a feline, with sleek subtle lines. My fingers slid
carefully across her smooth taut belly, along her ribs. The
swell of her breasts were even lovelier to behold than I had
imagined. I felt her nipples rise involuntarily as I flicked
them with the tips of her fingers.*
*Her cheek was soft, the bones of her neck delicate, her
collarbones incredibly exposed.*
*She tasted like a delicate flower. She must have showered
after her rehearsal because the scent of soap was still
redolent on her inside thighs. A sharp intake of breath told*

*me that she was either shocked into disbelief or incredibly
turned on.*

*When I entered her, she closed her eyes against what I could
only imagine was a growing affection. To say she was in love
with me, some would argue as premature, but if you had asked
me in that moment, I would have bet even money that she was
falling in love with me.*

*I drove her into the mattress like a beautiful splayed
butterfly, driving my penis deep inside her like a piston.
I was pretty certain that she was wet; I was sweating
profusely and some of it may have been dripping from my skin.
Hard to say.*

He left her spent on the frilly mattress, face down, soft
buttocks exposed. Her toes were so pink and unblemished as
they lay among the former knots of the sash. A light sheen of
his sweat covered her back and legs. His seed may already be
growing new life in her body. She could dance, he thought,
while a nanny watched their child.

He would call on her in the morning, he thought, as he left
her gently crying and softly closed the door. She would have
time to have processed it all, he felt, by morning. He would
take her out for eggs and they could begin to plan their
future together.

He was genuinely surprised when he found the police waiting
for him at his apartment when he got home.

-30-

THE HORNY GHOST
by "M"

The Horny Ghost
By Marni

Friday.
The airport, much like the D.C. area itself, was built like a
circular maze: difficult to navigate, impossible to exit.
After I said goodbye to Harry, I made a beeline for the car in
parking lot 7. Crowds gave me the heebie- jeebies, and big
holiday crowds scared me to death. After I climbed into our
little Nissan, I locked the doors and took a deep breath.

It was only Friday. Harry wouldn't be back until Monday, which
felt (from my vantage of this lonely parking lot) like an
eternity. Add that the girls were away for a camping weekend
with my brother's family, and you'd have a few days of rest
and peaceful quiet that any woman might envy.

Any woman but me.

The prospect of being alone in a great big house overlooking a
restive bay filled me with dread. Watching the leaden hours
pass before I fell into my husband's arms again left me cold.
What to do.
I could read of course; try a new hairstyle; bake. Put on
"You've Got Mail', make a big batch of popcorn, and enjoy a
good cry. The problem was, I was not in the mood to do any of
these things. I craved the laughter and camaraderie of my
family and THIS long, long weekend I was SOL (shit out of
luck!) in that department.

Resigned to a weekend as exciting as watching paint dry, I
started the car and pointed it in the direction of home.

The house looked empty as I approached the winding drive
through the woods. Emptier.

My house keys echoed disappointingly on the kitchen marble
counter. My heels clicked loudly on the polished wood floor.
"Hello, house," I said aloud to myself. The words sounded dull
and tinny in the oppressive silence. I suddenly felt very

lonely in the cavernous house. Without Harry and the kids, this weekend was going to drag.

I decided to treat myself to a luxurious bubble bath (then maybe, order takeout). That always seemed to be the way the heroine did it in the movies, right? I started the bath, then went into my bedroom to slip out of my confining business clothes and into my favorite soft blue bathrobe.

I could feel the tensions of the day dissipate as the bath water level rose. In a few moments a light steam hovered on the surface of the water. I disrobed quickly and slid into the warming tub. The water felt soothing and enervating the instant it began caressing my skin. I stretched my legs languidly under the water, while my nipples (at water level) were tickled by the undulating surface.

I smiled secretly as steam rose from the bath to layer my face and shoulders like a moist facecloth. Resting my neck and shoulders against the back of the tub, the cares of the day (and the prospect of a long empty weekend) seemed to melt away like lemon drops.

Invariably, my fingers stole south. With my eyes closed, I pretended they were Henry's fingers, tracing the outline of my hips, soothingly touching my legs.

As the water glistened against my bare skin, my fingers reached my secret spot. I peeled away the outer layers carefully to play with my clitoris.

A small electric wave of pleasure swept over me, and I closed my eyes tightly until it passed.

My fingertips moved stealthily over my pubic mound (mons venus, I remembered from high school health classes). I turned the water faucet handle with a light tap of my red-polished big toe; a thin cascade of warm water splashed down into my scented bath. I scooted my hips closer to the faucet, aligning myself perfectly with the steady stream.

The pulse of water on my aching cooze was indescribably hot. Supporting my upper body on my elbows, I threw my head back as a wave of sensual dizziness swept over me.

The pulse of water felt like a man's fat fingers as they massaged my pussy like bread dough. I surrendered to the feeling, shutting my eyes tightly as my orgasm began to build. Skin glistening, nipples feeling distended and very sensitive, I felt the "fingers" probing deeper, exploring.

Dimly, it began to dawn on me that these "magic fingers" were behaving like a real man's hand and not at all like an inanimate stream of water!

Someone or something was finger fucking me for real! Reluctantly breaking the spell I was under, I tried to pull myself to a sitting position in the tub. I know this sounds crazy but I felt a strong hand push me back roughly. I was so surprised that I swallowed just a bit of warm bathwater.

Reaching down, my hands closed around a man's wrist, intent on helping me reach orgasm!

My eyes opened wide to see my white bathrobe hanging from the wall - but no one else in the room!

I held onto the "wrist", grinding involuntarily against the imaginary hand as a powerful orgasm swept over me. I shut my eyes tightly against the spasm, arching my back in the water. Bathwater sloshed against the sides of the tub as my orgasm coursed through my limbs like electricity.

After I calmed down, I started to laugh. I must have needed it because I had made up a whole internal scenario involving a "man". What disturbed me (a little) was the whole 'forced against my will' aspect of the deed. I shrugged into my white robe after toweling off. What difference did it really make, I thought, as long as nobody got hurt.?

Besides, it had been a long while since Harry had delivered a rocking orgasm. I was overdue!

&&&&

I caught up on some TV shows I'd missed when Harry and the girls took me to Washington. My not so secret guilty pleasures were the various Housewife shows from around the country, but I also enjoyed some of the crime shows too.

The white plush robe felt luxuriant against my cool skin. I stretched my legs languidly out on the sofa., admiring my latest pedi. Soft pink, I felt, was the color of innocence. Opening my robe and pushing my legs further across the soft cushions of the sofa, I lay my head back against the soft rounded couch arm. Lying open and naked in a lighted room felt strangely sensual. My cool fingers crept like a spider down the length of my flat stomach and down across my hips.

My mons venus rose like a small rollercoaster, cresting at the opening for my slightly distended clitoris. I kneaded my clit between the thumb and forefinger of my right hand . With my left, I played with the pink nipples of my left breast.

I imagined Harry's brother Frank had stopped by our house and found the front door open. He had wandered from room to room, hat in hand, looking for signs of life until he came across the sight of me, quite unexpectedly, sleeping on the sofa in the nude.

Frank watched me for awhile, enjoying the curves and softness of my skin. Then he began to disrobe.

His eyes played over my bare breasts as he advanced to the couch. I'd seen Frank many times at picnics and pool parties and I was familiar with his hard, lean-muscled body. I was unprepared for my first glimpse of his unsheathed cock, which was rigid now and had a slight curve upward.

In my fevered imagination, Frank knelt beside the couch and slowly opened my legs. He traced the soft line of my vaginal opening, first with his eyes and then with the feather soft touch of his fingers.

Leaning forward, my "brother in law" tasted my cunt with the small pink tip of his tongue. Placing his hands on either side of my thighs, he gently opened my labia, running his tongue the full length of my opening. I threw my hand back on the couch as I lay there, splayed open for the world to see, while Frank ate my sopping pussy.

My eyes rolled up in their sockets as I arched my pelvis toward "Frank's" eager tongue. Waves of pleasure rolled through my body like the pulse of an ocean's ebb against the shore.

Pink met pink as his tongue (whoever's tongue felt so damned insistently hungry as the sensation felt even more real now) dug deeper into my aching loins.

Arching my back, I lifted my hips to meet his ravenous mouth. I felt light-headed and swoozy as the ceiling began to turn. I held fast to the couch cushions as I clenched my hips against an orgasm of titanic dimensions.

"OH - MY- GOD!" I screamed aloud in the cavernous room. My own voice returned with a slight echo.

My tan legs were splayed in opposite directions, my pink toenail polish taunting me like a child's cotton-candy.

I felt like Dorothy Gale, returned from Oz to earth again with a surprised "oh!".

Where did that come from?

I couldn't quite shake the feeling that this was not totally my own sub-conscious energy. It felt (and we're veering into supernatural territory) like some other-worldly power had rendered me helpless and vulnerable.

It wasn't entirely unexpected or even a bad feeling, but I definitely felt 'forced' to orgasm.

&&&&

I had a light snack of fruit and yogurt, and tried to relax with something on TV. But it had been a draining evening (pun intended) and I decided to go to bed early.

The sheets felt cool against my bare skin as I slid between them, turning the light off and snuggling into my favorite pillows. The house was still and quiet as a church, and the large picture window showed my glittering pool under a full luminescent moon.

Normally I liked to sleep with the windows open, but I was reticent until Frank was home again. I may have been sleeping moments or hours when I woke again.

The moon still clung to a black sky, in a slightly changed position outside; but now my arms and legs had been tied to the four posts of the bed.

I realized with an odd mixture of fear and delight that this was clearly not a dream. I also knew (in my heart of hearts) that this was not a total surprise.

There was a real spirit at play here, I'd sensed it from the first time I gripped his wrist in the bathtub , and he wanted me badly.

I heard footsteps in the hall: heavy, dragging, like Old Marley's ghost. Harry had come back early from his trip, I thought with a brief smile playing over my red lips. That had to be it. He was playing tricks on me, I was sure of it.

I would have added clanking chains, I thought giddily as the noise grew louder. Right outside my bedroom door , the footfalls suddenly stopped. I heard them scuffing on the wooden floor as the "ghost" turned toward me.

"Ok, Harry," I said, trying to keep my voice even. Although I did my best to disguise my excitement, I was beginning to feel giddy and light-headed with anticipation. The restraints were tight, and my wrists and ankles strained at their tight confinement. The first order of the night, I decided, as soon as Harry disrobed of course , would be to loosen my silk bondage.

The rapping began on the door. Loud, insistent. When the door finally swung open, revealing the space in the hall to be empty, I have to admit I was surprised.

Harry was not the creative type. This time he had clearly outdone himself.

The "steps" drew closer to the bed. I could feel cool air tingle my bare skin as I strained in

the grey light to see. But there was nothing to see. The "footsteps" reached the end of my bed. Someone touched my foot - lovingly, caressing my instead, kneading my toes between thumb and forefinger.

This was crazy. There was no one there! I was dreaming! That had to be it, I must be dreaming.

I felt a hand running lightly along my ankle. But it couldn't be real. I closed my eyes as this 'disembodied hand' worked its way up my leg. I confess to getting a warm feeling as it reached my thigh. My vaginal lips pulsed as it suddenly appeared on my opposite thigh. Running in no particular hurry down the other leg. Was the hand cold or warm? It was too hard to tell.

Enough moonlight still shone in the room to make out indefinite shapes: a bureau, a stand-alone mirror, a chair. I could glimpse a small portion of the bed frame from the mirror, but I didn't see anyone hiding or even the occasional shadow at play. It was as if there was someone there - and I tell you, there was! - but it would be impossible to prove.

I felt my other-worldly guest now up near my ear, breathing warm air across the nape of my neck. I could sense ragged breathing (other than my own!).

That's when I felt the mattress shift. A weight was applied to one side of the bed, and someone - some thing - was climbing over me. I felt a man's weight as he lay atop me. His chest felt hard and rugged as he pressed it against mine. His legs pushed mine open just a bit more as he readied himself to penetrate me.

He teased my vaginal lips open with the head of his penis, pushing his turgid manhood inside me like a sword returned to its sheath.

No prelude, no foreplay, no drama. Not that I wasn't fully aroused already! I took him completely inside – slowly, achingly – until our hips clapped together. This was still quite an odd sensation as all I could see above me was thin air. While I felt a man moving inside me, the weight pinning me down on the mattress and splaying my legs like a holiday turkey, there appeared to be no one else in the room but me. His cock pummeled me as I lay there, helpless. I could hear the wet sounds of my sopping clit but I felt imperiled to hang on for dear life as every fiber of my soul coaxed semen from (I could only imagine) his straining love tube.

"Yes- yes!!" I coaxed him on. "Harder. Harder."

His thrusts quickened as he pinned me like a beautiful butterfly to the mattress. I could feel my own orgasm building as my hips pushed forward to meet his throbbing tool. His penis was long and the girth was good, and I could feel it beginning to pulse. Any moment, and his cannon would release itself deep inside me.

I think "he" could feel that too, because he changed rhythm. He began to slow down, finally pulling himself from my lips and laying heavily across me as his breathing returned to normal again.

I must have fallen asleep because when I woke – moments? hours? – later, he was no longer on top of me.

The silk ties that had held me fast were also gone.

I fell asleep again, this time greatly disappointed.

&&&&&

When I woke, my face was buried in a pillow and "he" was back, this time entering me from behind. My hands reached out for purchase as he lifted my pelvis and fucked me doggie style. It had been years since Harry did that!

I caught my breath and tried to look around. I was unsurprised to find that the dawn was slowly creeping back, and of course that there was still no one else in the room! Shapes of furniture were beginning to grow more distinct. The mirror was still bare, except for the sight of me being forcibly taken by thin air.

This time I wasn't dreaming!

His penis felt rock-hard as he drove himself into me. Over and over again, I gasped for air as he seemed to be drive it out of my body with every violent thrust of his tool. I was impaled on his cock and loving every minute of it.

Suddenly I was on my side, right leg thrown over an imaginary shoulder as he drove through my pussy like a hot knife in butter. One hand on my leg, the other firmly across my taut stomach, I could feel the light-headed feeling returning. My vagina ached as I could feel his sperm building inside his massive organ. The first wave of my orgasm rolled over me like the crashing surf as our genitals thrummed with delicious anticipation. I knew there was more to cum, I thought, smiling at the pun as my ghostly man flipped me onto my back.

He lifted my pelvis easily and I could see my vaginal lips opening and closing around thin air as he explored every inch of me with that magnificent cock! "I'm going to cum again!" I shouted, which felt pretty stupid in an empty room and this one - THIS time - warm liquid shot out of me like cannon fire. Wave upon wave of orgasm dribbled from my sopping lips as I struggled for air. Eyes and teeth clenched tightly, I rolled my head against the pillow.

This was one feeling I did not want to EVER stop.

He came inside me: I could feel the warm liquid splash against the pink walls of my vaginal barrel as our juices mixed together. His fingers gripped my legs tighter as he clenched inside me , trying unsuccessfully to stop the flow of who knows how many decades of dormancy.

I must have been day-dreaming because the next time I focused on my window, the dawn was coming up - pink and orange on the wet grass outside.

I struggled to pull myself up on the mattress, toes searching for my slippers.

Time for a bath, I thought happily: and whatever pleasures I would find waiting for me in there.

END

CAMP SLEEP-AWAY

AN EROTIC SHORT BY MARNIE

Camp Sleep Away

By Marnie

August always makes me wistful. It seems like everything is
coming to an end. The golden promise of summer fades to the
harsh reality of a new school year. Trees turn color, flowers
wilt, beach crowds fade away to a stalwart few.
Camp Sleep-away was no exception.
Holly and I had been going to the Camp since we were knee high
to a grasshopper. We both watched the camp grow from three
camp leaders ro a staff of nineteen counselors.
We saw kids grow during the summer in confidence as well as
height; shy timid kids
 who started with us in June left taller and more sure of
themselves by summer's end.
Lifelong bonds were formed under the maypole and around the
late-night campfires
 of Camp Sleep-away. Certainly while most of our other friends
stayed home and
wished their summers away, my friendship with Holly -
already close to begin with -
was forged in the fire of 'smores and hot dogs.
Summer passed, and only a skeleton crew remained on our little
island camp. While we were both anxious to get on with college
and family, we were reluctant to say goodbye so quickly. Max
was a new counselor. I was a bit jealous by how quickly he and
Holl seemed to hit it off. Whenever I looked for a friend to
watch a scary movie with, or to tell campfire stories to the
kids, Holly and Max were off somewhere kanoodling! I guess it
was only inevitable that one or the other of us would meet a
good-looking boy: we were both pretty hot looking ourselves,
if I do say so myself!
Still, there was an innocence about camp that seemed to
preclude boys and romance. Camp Sleep-away had always been our
guilty pleasure. Sitting around in our panties and tees doing
our nails and gossiping, or just watching a corny television
show - the camp had always been our special together place.
Suddenly I was feeling again like a third wheel, and very
anxious to get on with my real life and button up the camp for
another season.
Who knows, I sulked in our cabin on the next to last night;
maybe this would be my last season at Sleep-away. I was 18
now, no longer a child. Maybe I would get a real job next
summer at a store or someplace, make a real paycheck. The sun

went down quickly this night and dark clouds moved across the island, perfectly capturing my mood.

Holly stamped in shortly before 7, holding a yellow plastic poncho over her head.

"Is it raining?" I said , trying to mask my hurt.

"Starting to," she said. "Just enough to mess up my hair."

She began stomping around our cabin apartment, kicking her shoes and jeans off angrily, grabbing a hairbrush and scraping it violently across her scalp. "I am so pissed right now at Max," she volunteered. " I could spit nails."

"What happened?" I said, looking up from the tv.

"He stood me up. I waited for him for almost an hour down by the food court. I finally stamped over to his quarters and he was sleeping. He admitted that he had been out all afternoon with that skank Dani, and was so tired he flopped into bed with setting his alarm for our date."

"You're kidding!" I managed.

"If only I was. I broke up with him right there and then, on the spot."

"Were you two exclusive?"

"No idea. I felt like we were. It doesn't matter though. I gave that bastard his walking papers!"

"You sound like you're in serious need of some tea," I said brightly, rising from the bed where I had plopped for the night and continuing to the stove.

"If you put a little whiskey in it, you've got yourself a deal. I need something a little stronger tonight."

Holly tended to exaggerate, I thought. This would all be blown over in an hour.

"I was just about to crash with a romantic weeper," I said. "Care to do a little Sleepless in Seattle?"

"How about Kill Bill?" she said. "Only we substitute Max's name!"

She giggled. She was coming back. Holly got comfortable in light blue cotton tee and panties while I popped some corn.

"You're overdressed!" she giggled, as I pulled off my shorts and we climbed under a blanket on the couch. I balanced the popcorn bowl on the small blanket mountain on our laps and pointed the remote at the tv.

"Just like old times," I said, stuffing the buttery kernels in my mouth.

"I'm swearing off men altogether!" said Holly. "From now on, its lez all the way!"

"You'd make a terrible lesbian," I said. "Max spoiled you with his 'perfect cock'."

"It was only perfect when it was pumping into me," she said. "Now since he turned jerk, I hope it turns black and drops off!"

For some reason, we both thought that was funny and dissolved in a new round of giggles.

"How do I know if I'll like my new lifestyle though? I've never kissed a girl before."

You could have knocked me over with a feather. For a brief uncomfortable moment we looked into each other's eyes. Hers were like blue liquid and beautiful. In a second, we were kissing!

I hugged her tightly. Sometimes the only thing you can do is hug. Her firm breasts felt wonderful through our thin shirts. I could tell that her nipples were small and pointed.

She leaned into me, forcing me lightly to my side of the couch as she lay over me. Our lips
remained locked as she stretched her body against mine. I couldn't believe this was happening!

Holly's hands began to explore my arms and upper body. Her hand moved to my stomach and I began to get little butterflies as she reached under my shirt. Her hand moved higher to lightly cup my breast. All while this was happening our tongues played, exploring each other's mouths. I sucked on her tongue as she kneaded my nipple between her thumb and forefinger. "Take off your shirt," she demanded as we each gasped for air.

We both undressed quickly. Slipping my panties off, I felt weird but excited under the thin blanket. We continued to explore with our hands as we kissed. Her hand moved down to my waist. I gasped as her fingers played over my glistening vaginal lips.

Suddenly I was aware that we weren't alone. I'd forgotten that her dopey boyfriend Max had a key to our room, and he was standing there with a leer on his lips as he watched.

I gasped and pointed with my chin. "What the hell are you doing here?" she said. "Isn't the skank available?"

"Don't mind me, ladies. Please continue," said Max, as he pulled a chair to the edge of the couch..

"Fuck him," Holly shrugged, kissing me now with more urgency. She dipped two fingers into my vagina and I felt my head drop back as a wave of ecstasy passed over me. I think the fact that Max was watching - somehow - made it all the more exciting!

Gradually the blanket fell away and he had an excellent view of my pussy as Holly pumped her fingers into my sopping lips. "Oh -God," I moaned. "Holly."

Before I realized what was happening, Max had slipped to his knees and was holding open my legs as he licked me with his hard insistent tongue. I could feel the stubble of his chin on my thighs.

As he continued to eat me out, Holly moved from the bed. She had unzipped her boyfriend's pants and began to lick his semi-flaccid cock. Max half-rose to his feet, lifting me up with both hands under my buttocks as he continued to lick me to orgasm.

My head rolled against the pillow while I cupped my breasts,
my legs and pelvis dangling in mid-air while Max tasted my
flowing juices. "So-o good," I said, my eyes fluttering as my
pelvis thrummed against his open taunting mouth.
He dropped me to the couch and half-lifted Holly to her feet.
She had licked and sucked Max to his usual rigid self, and he
threw her on the mattress face-down. When he entered her from
behind, Holly's mouth flew open but no words came out.
The only sound in the room now was his heavy breathing and the
slap of their skin as he pistoned his pelvis into her doggy-
style.
"I don't like that skank," he said between thrusts.
"Fuck you both," said Holly, sticking to her guns even as his
thick engorged cock pummeled her to senselessness. I laid
under her and began to lick her nipples, feeling very much the
outsider now as I felt them harden under my small pink tongue.
From my new curious perch, I could see Max's balls slapping
against Holly's shaved mound. His dick glistened as he drove
it hard into his girlfriend's tasty gash.
She was at the point of no return now, and I doubled my
efforts on her tits. As she hunched into a thundering orgasm,
gripping the blanket and tightening her eyes against wave upon
wave of pleasure, Max pulled his cock out of her dripping
pussy and grunted.
"Come here," he said, pulling me by my hair and coming against
my mouth. Hot sperm fell across my teeth and I tasted Max. His
milky semen was slightly salty and I couldn't get enough.
He dragged us both by our arms over to the bed. Holly
protested mildly but he pushed his dick against her teeth.
"Suck me back," he said gruffly. He began kissing me and
running his hands roughly over my breasts. "Not bad," he said
appreciatively. "You're gonna watch for a while. I'll let you
know when I'm ready for you."
I began to tell him what he could do with himself, when he
raised his hand like he was going to strike me. "I can't take
her lip," he said. "I'm sure as hell not going to take yours."
I settled into a corner of the mattress, my legs crossed as I
sulked. He seemed to be hard in no time as Holly licked him
back into full hard working order again. He stood beside the
mattress as he splayed her legs with his arms and rubbed the
head of his penis against her moistened clit.
The scene was so erotic that I played with myself
surreptitiously as he explored her vaginal barrel an inch at a
time.
"Sit on her face," Max ordered.
"What?" I said, more curious than pissed off.
"Don't make me say it again!" he demanded.
As I squatted on my best friend's face, I could feel her
tongue timidly exploring my sensitive pink walls. She was
growing bolder as her own excitement began to kick into hyper-
drive again. Max slid his cock easily inside Holly's pussy:

in, out, in, out. Her tongue drove deeper into my sopping slice as Max kissed me over his girlfriend's writhing body. When she came - and she came fairly quickly - Holly hummed and shrieked into my pelvis. I could feel the rhythm building in the dripping walls of my vaginal barrel as my pussy thrummed with her screaming orgasm and began to build to a climax of its own.

Max pulled me off his girlfriend's face. He placed a pillow under my pelvis as he entered me missionary style. My ankles embraced his strong hunched back, my hands found his bulging biceps as he drove his cock into me like a jackhammer.

Over and over Max pushed his thick cock into me. Holly appeared to have fallen asleep in a corner of the bed as he pistoned into me like a machine. Time seemed to stand still as the room swayed and we floated on air.

"Your pussy is so tight," Max grunted as my pink lips slipped and tightened against his turgid flesh. "I'm gonna cum!! "

I was too but I didn't want to give him the satisfaction of knowing he made me cum twice. Suddenly his body tensed, and his rigid cock jumped and twitched inside my cunt as hot semen blasted me with its gooey goodness. I could feel our juices blending as I held him tighter and my abdominal muscles jerked involuntarily as we both came together.

"That was pretty good," he said. "Give me 15 minutes, and we'll do it again."

The three of us fucked into the night. Sometimes it was just Max and me. Sometimes he took on Holly and ignored me. Sometimes we let him sleep and explored our bodies together: Holly and I fingering each other to climax, or scissoring each other until our pussies burst wet against each other.

I felt close to her in those moments; as our hot breath slowed and we lay beside each other, brushing the hair out of our faces, tracing our nipples in the dark with our curious fingers.

I don't know if it was all a big set-up. A fake fight, everything.

I guess it doesn't really matter.

Whatever happened that late August night in the woods , it was a memorable cap to an amazing summer. I still smile privately when I think of the things we did, and I can still pleasure myself at the erotic memory of our three young bodies intertwined in bed.

-30-

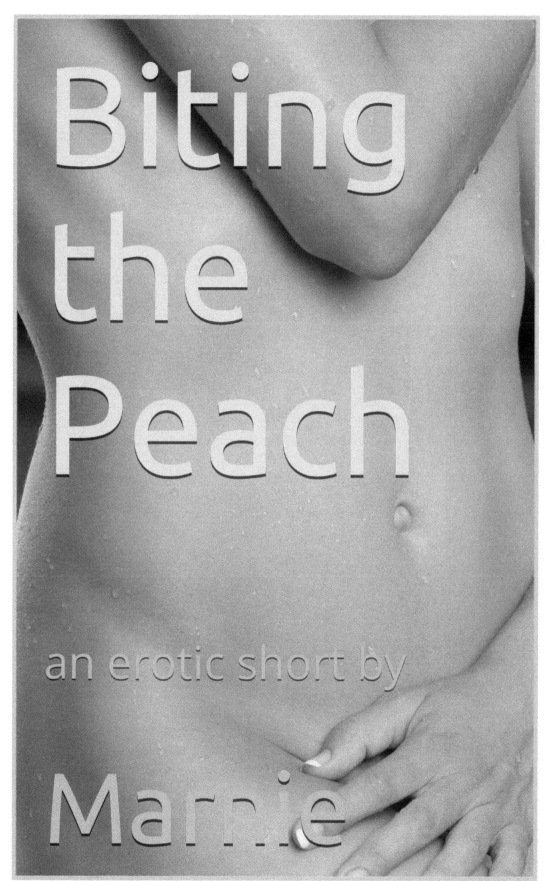

Biting the Peach

an erotic short by

Marnie

BITING THE PEACH
By Marnie   f/f

So…
I'd thought about girls, I'd be lying if I told you otherwise.
I'd watched classmates soaping their nubile bodies under the
shower after swim class. Tan skin, perfect globular breasts,
while rivulets of soapy water ran down their taut, flawless
stomachs.
On those crazy afternoons, I ached to reach over to touch my
friend Alyne's smooth back, to caress her slender shoulder
blades, to taste the lobe of her ear with the pointy tip of my
pink tongue.
To watch her eyes slowly close as her head fell back
involuntarily, the water cascading over both our naked bodies.
Much as I wanted to feel Alyne up under the shower, in full
view of all our classmates, I resisted.
I resisted.
Besides, all we talked about were boys. What if she rebuffed
my crude advance and it seriously affected our friendship?
What if it got around school that I was a dyke?
Because I wasn't, not at all. But there was something about
Alyne that I was drawn to. She was incredibly sexy, almost
unconsciously so. When she sipped her drink through a straw,
or was complaining to me about her evil step-father. I watched
her pout her lips.
When we cuddled at sleepovers, the sweet smell of her hair was
intoxicating. I would hold her close under the covers, feeling
her bosom rise and fall against mine as our long legs
intertwined.
When she cried at her grandmother's wake, I was there to
console her and brush away her tears.
In Senior year, I got my first boyfriend before Alyne did. It
ended at the same time as hers began. Boys came and went with
surprising regularity, but our bond always remained strong.
We were accepted at the same college, talked about sharing a
dorm together. I'm not sure why I was so reticent about living
together: it may have been the same reason couples are
reluctant to move in.
Familiarity breeds contempt, isn't that the popular saying? My
friendship with Alyne was so close, perhaps I just didn't
want to monkey with the formula.
After a week, she knocked at my door with two bags packed and
an ultimatum. If I didn't let her move in with me this very
night , she would be on the news tomorrow, charged with her
roommate's murder!

Alyne moved in completely by the next morning. She kept me
regaled with horrific tales of stinky socks and endless
telephone marathons. She pushed her bed against the opposite
wall so we could talk late into the nights. And we did!

%%%

We both slept in colored panties and white tees; always had,
ever since our first sleepover. So it was natural to see Alyne
padding around our room in pink or blue undies, her long tan
legs with comfortable cotton or woolen socks. Sometimes I came
back from Study Hall to find her rummaging through my drawers
because we both wore the same sizes. "Do you mind?" she'd say,
caught red-handed. "Mine are in the laundry."
I never minded.

%%%

Too much snow spoiled my plans to fly home over the Christmas
holidays. I didn't tell my roomie because she seemed so
excited at the prospect of seeing her family. Instead, I
pretended to have a last-minute cold, sitting around with wads
of Kleenex and a DVD of The Way We Were.
I encouraged Alyne not to think of me at all. Her parents had
moved to Florida and that flight had not been cancelled.
"Enjoy yourself," I said between convincing "blows". "Before
you know it, two weeks will be up."
In truth, I felt miserable about the prospect of spending two
weeks alone without my BFF.
But I didn't want her to know that, or change her plans at
all.
I wished Alyne a very Merry Christmas and "air kissed" her
goodbye. She left in a blur of suitcases and anxiety. Later I
checked online to see that her flight- despite the heavy wet
snow - had left without a hitch and landed safely.

%%%

Steisand was brushing Redford's hair back from his forehead,
and I was a wreck. No matter how many times I watched this
classic, the ending always got me.
I grabbed my towel and made a beeline for the girl's shower,
which was across the hall. The dorm was deserted - I felt like
the only loser whose flight had been cancelled.
"Hello?" I said to the empty hall. It was strange to see this
normally bustling floor empty and silent as a tomb.
There was nothing like a luxuriant warm shower after a good
cry, I thought as I quickly undressed. Especially on a night
with chilly wet snow outside. I started the shower and felt
the spray with the palm of my hand.

When I was satisfied that the temperature was just right, I ventured my left foot under the shower. The misadventures of Hubbell and Katie, and my profound emptiness at being alone on the holidays, seemed to melt away like Frosty in summer as the soothing warm water caressed my skin.

I closed my eyes as I melted under the spray. Water coursed my cheeks, ran in heavy rivulets across my full breasts and down my legs.

It was ironic that I'd just had my toes painted a beautiful red as now they would only be seen by my television screen.

My hands unconsciously played over my supple breasts. My pink nipples began to harden under my soapy fingers like small diamonds -

"I can do that better," said Alyne, cupping my tits with her hands.

I was so startled that my eyes snapped open. She was standing behind me, completely - spectacularly - nude. My mouth fell open and Alyne covered it with hers.

"Your flight?" I said breathlessly.

"And leave my bestie alone at Christmas?"

"You left hours ago-" I protested weakly.

"Ever look for a good Chinese restaurant in the snow?" said Alyne.

She held my head in her hands, kissing me passionately as my hands caressed her soft shoulders. "I've been wanting to kiss you for years," I confessed as we broke for air.

"You don't think I knew that?" said Alyne.

Her lips moved lower, to the side of my neck. As my head lolled back, surrendering to her small passionate kisses, an involuntary moan escaped my lips. No longer embarrassed, giving myself to the moment, I held the sides of Alyne's breasts in my hands. They were firm yet soft, and soapy water ran down my hands and across her flat belly. Her beautiful rose-colored nipples hardened as I kneaded them between thumb and forefinger.

Her sensuous lips moved to my left breast. She teased my tit with her tongue, cupping my entire areola with her entire mouth. Her hands had dropped to my butt as she took me into her warm eager mouth.

When she moaned, I could feel the vibration throughout my chest wall. Her hands pulled me closer as her right leg slipped between both of mine.

She began to work her thigh against my slick pussy lips, grinding her leg into my cooze as I held onto her shoulders for dear life!

As I got the hang of it, my right leg rubbed Alyne's shaved pussy, both of us 'scissoring' each other to a shuddering climax. Her breath came in short, stuttering bursts as she rested her chin near my ear.

"That was worth the wait," I said as my own ragged breathing slowed enough to speak.

"My dear," Alyne said with a knowing smile, " we've only just begun -. "

%%%

My friend toweled me off with a fluffy white towel, taking considerable care on my breast and pussy. She led me by the hand to the wide oak bench that faced the gray metal lockers. After spreading another soft towel across the wood bench, she directed me to lie down on my back, looking up at the bright lights overhead.

My legs were wide open, straddling the oak bench, with my pussy exposed. Alyne also straddled the bench, sitting up near my knees. She knelt over my pelvis, spreading my labia with her thumbs, breathing hotly into my wet aching hole.

I wasn't prepared for the jolt of electricity her tongue caused as she stretched it full-length inside me. My breath sharpened as she tasted my dripping cunt. She was slow but insistent, using a short darting method as she explored the walls of my pink sugar tube.

"OH- GOD!" I cried out involuntarily as Alyne's mouth covered my slit completely.

My hands entwined in her golden hair, pressing her face closer to my eager pussy lips. My pelvis lifted from the wood bench to meet her educated tongue.

Licking her fingers, Alyne introduced her slender right index and middle finger into my wet box; working them in and out as I writhed with pleasure.

She continued to flick her tongue against my distended clit as she pumped me with her fingers. I swooned under the bright overhead lights as the walls of my cooze began to thrum with anticipation. My orgasm began to build as she reached up to squeeze my melons. My breath was coming fast as I arched my pelvis and clenched my teeth together. My hands reached out for purchase as a shuddering climax racked my shapely body.

Alyne seemed to be enjoying my taste as she searched my cavern for more sweet honey. She kissed her way up the length of my body and then smiled as she reached my mouth. My eyes must have looked at her gratefully as I lay there, drenched in a thin sheen of sweat and totally drained of energy.

"I just want to sleep against you," I said softly.

"Not so fast," she said, taking control once again. She stood up and pulled me to a sitting position on the bench. "Let's go, young lady. We're not finished by a long shot!"

%%%%%

We fell into each other's arms in my bed, back in the dorm. This time, with the door locked and the music turned up slightly, even a straggler wandering through the dorm offered no distraction.

Alyne and I hugged for a long time. Her breath smelled like candy and her skin was warm and soft as we caressed each other's shoulders and back. Her fingers felt cool and knowing as they traced a line along my arms, or brushed away hair from my forehead.

Her lips felt feather-soft on mine. We must have kissed for an hour. Soft, wet tongues probing each other's mouths, tracing the other's lips.

I experimented by touching side boob. She responded by cupping mine. Since we had similar athletic bodies, I was sure we complemented each other. My lips traveled to the soft hollow of her neck. Before long, I was moving down her body - first on her tits, giving equal time to each nipple. Feeling them harden like small chocolate drops as I circled each areola with the tip of my tongue.

My tongue tasted her belly button , which was just a slit. As I worked my way across her smooth flat belly, and began to tease her clit apart with my mouth, I heard Alyne moan and her legs parted.

I lay between them, spreading her soft thighs as I tasted her pussy for the first time. She rested her heels on my shoulders as I licked her clit. Up and down, side to side. I even tried a small trick I read about spelling the alphabet on her labia in case I got bored.

I was NOT bored!

She thrashed against the mattress like she was in throes of a deep ecstasy. I could feel her clitoris hardening in my mouth. "Don't stop, don't stop, don't," Alyne grunted as the first massive wave of her orgasm arrived. "I'm cumming!" she announced to no one, a little surprised herself. Then he closed her eyes tightly and rocked her head against the pillow.

She tried to push my head away but I doubled my efforts. My arms held her to the mattress, pinned with her legs splayed open like a beautiful butterfly. Her body went rigid as the second wave swept through her like an electric current.

I could taste the floods of Lake Alyne as she soaked the mattress with her love.

"That was amazing," she whispered hoarsely as I sat up in front of her and scissored our legs so that as we gently rocked, our pussies ground together with soft slurping sounds. I started slowly, holding her right knee against my chest for leverage as my lips rubbed against hers. Electric waves of energy seemed to pass through our most intimate of parts as we rubbed our taco's together. The pace quickened as our excitement reached fever pitch until we were literally slapping against each other. It felt as if I were being pummeled by the world's smartest invisible cock as I watched my beautiful friend writhe and thrash against the clean white sheets.

From my vantage point, I had a great view of the action and I
could see the slick threads of cum as we separated and then
came together again. We exploded together and I fell across my
friend's body. I could feel her heart beating quickly as we
breathed into each other's mouths and after-shocks of cum made
us quake and tremor for several minutes.
I rolled off Alyne and stared at the ceiling.
I heard the clock down the hall gonging lightly over the
Christmas sounds of our radio. "It's past midnight," I said.
"Merry Christmas," she smiled.
We both giggled.

%%%%

In the morning, she introduced some toys she'd brought. We
took turns masturbating for each other, and then with each
other. We licked and tasted and humped and finger-fucked most
of the next morning. While the rest of the world opened
presents, we were busy opening each other.
But mostly we just held each other and rocked ourselves to
sleep. "Because that's what friends do," Alyne said with a
wicked giggle.

END

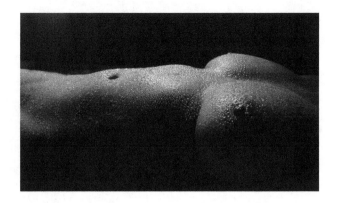

Thank you for joining us this sultry evening. Please join us
soon for more exciting Marnie product…
Until then, pleasant dreams..